THE GREAT PICTURE HUNT

HEY, WALDO FANS, WELCOME TO THE GREAT PICTURE HUNT. IT'S MORE THAN A BOOK — IT'S AN ART ADVENTURE! THE FUN STARTS ON THE NEXT PAGE, IN OLDAW'S PICTURE PANDEMONIUM, WHERE YOU'LL FIND 30 ENORMOUS PORTRAITS. EXAMINE THEM CAREFULLY, PICTURE PERUSERS, BECAUSE EACH ONE OF THE PORTRAIT SUBJECTS CAN BE FOUND SOMEWHERE ELSE IN THIS BOOK.

STARTING WITH THE VERY FIRST EXHIBIT, AND ENDING WITH EXHIBIT 11, YOUR CHALLENGE IS TO FIND THESE SLIPPERY SUBJECTS WHEREVER THEY MAY BE HIDING! AND OF COURSE, BESIDES OUR FRANTIC FRAME GAME, THERE ARE ALL THE USUAL SUBJECTS AND THEIR LOST OBJECTS TO SPOT IN EVERY SCENE.

BUT THE BUZZER DOESN'T SOUND THERE, BECAUSE THERE ARE ADDED TWISTS LIKE SPOT-THE-DIFFERENCES PUZZLES. AND AT THE BACK OF THE BOOK, YOU'LL FIND CHALLENGING CHECKLISTS OF MORE THINGS TO FIND!

NOW, GALLERY GAZERS, HAVE FUN, DON'T MAKE AN EXHIBITION OF YOURSELVES, AND LET THE GREAT PICTURE HUNT BEGIN!

Waldo

FIND:

WALDO — OUR YOUNG GALLERY GUIDE, WHO TRAVELS EVERYWHERE!

WOOF — WHO WAGS HIS NOT-SO-BRUSH-LIKE TAIL (WHICH IS ALL YOU CAN SEE!).

WENDA — WHO TAKES THE PICTURES (BUT DOESN'T PAINT THEM!).

WIZARD WHITEBEARD — THE OLD MASTER, WHO CASTS COLORFUL SPELLS!

ODLAW — WHO'S BEEN AN EXHIBIT IN MANY A ROGUE'S GALLERY!

AND DON'T FORGET MY LOST KEY, WOOF'S MISSING BONE, WENDA'S MISPLACED CAMERA, WIZARD WHITEBEARD'S MISLAID SCROLL, AND ODLAW'S ABSENT BINOCULARS.

EXHIBIT 1 — ODLAW'S PICTURE PANDEMONIUM

WOW, WALDO FANS, WHAT PORTRAIT PANDEMONIUM! HAVE YOU EVER SEEN SO MANY YELLOW AND BLACK STRIPES IN ONE PLACE? STRIPETASTIC! WE'RE HERE IN ODLAW'S PICTURE GALLERY, AND JUST LOOK AT WHAT HIS ARTFUL ASSOCIATES HAVE CARRIED IN — 30 PECULIAR PORTRAITS IN AN ODDITY OF FRAMES. AMAZING! THERE'S QUITE A CAST OF CHARACTERS IN THESE PAINTINGS, AND THEY ALL APPEAR AGAIN ELSEWHERE IN THE BOOK. AND PICTURE THIS: ONE OF THEM EVEN APPEARS SOMEWHERE IN THIS CRAZY CROWD! GOOD LUCK ON YOUR HUNT FOR THE PLACES WITH THE FACES. WHAT A PICTURE!

EXHIBIT 2 —
A SPORTING LIFE
WELCOME, PICTURE HUNT PALS, TO MY
SPECIAL REPORT FROM THE LAND OF
SPORTS. FANTASTIC! IT'S LIKE THE OLYMPICS
EVERY DAY HERE, BUT WITH SO MANY
ATHLETIC EVENTS ON THE MENU, THERE'S NO
TIME LEFT FOR ANY REST AND RELAXATION.
BUT THERE'S NOTHING TOO STRENUOUS
ABOUT OUR MAIN EVENT, THE GREAT
PICTURE HUNT, SO KEEP YOUR EYES ON
THE BALL AND YOUR POINTER
FINGER READY. ON YOUR
MARK, GET SET, GO!

EXHIBIT 5 — THE PINK PARADISE PARTY

IT'S SATURDAY NIGHT, THE TEMPERATURE IS RISING, AND IT LOOKS AS IF A RASH OF MUSICAL MAYHEM AND DISCO FEVER HAS BROKEN OUT IN THIS DIZZY DANCE HALL. WHEW! IT'S HOT! HIP HIP-HOPPERS, ROCK-AND-ROLLERS, AND BODY-AND-SOULERS — IT'S A PACKED-OUT, PARTYGOERS' PINK PARADISE. SO GET ON DOWN, CUT YOUR GROOVE, AND MAKE YOUR MOVES — IT'S TIME TO SHUFFLE YOUR FEET TO THE PICTURE HUNT BEAT!

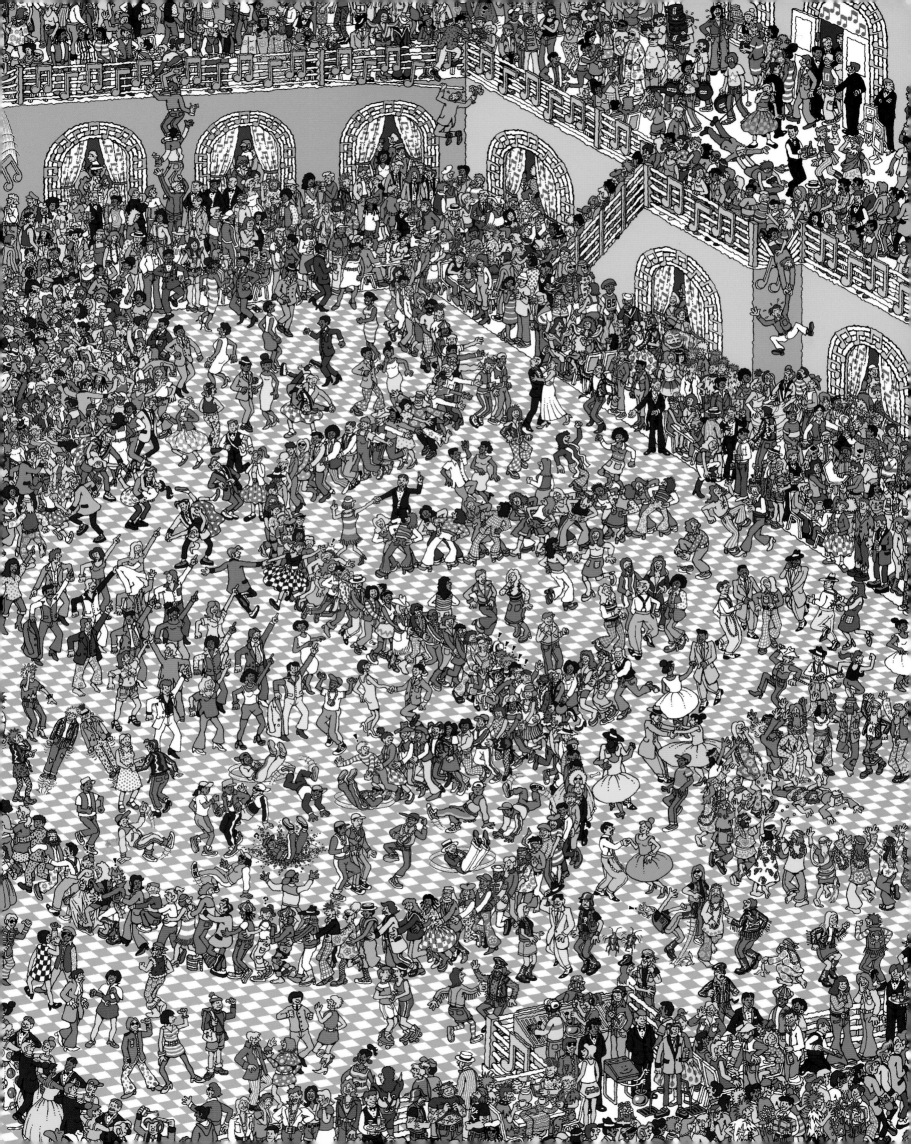

EXHIBIT 6 — OLD FRIENDS

AH, PICTURE HUNT PALS, HOW I LOVE TO LOOK THROUGH MY SCRAPBOOKS OF MEMORIES AND SOUVENIRS. THIS PAGE IS ONE OF MY FAVORITES: A COLLAGE CRAMMED WITH FAMILIAR FACES FROM MY EARLIER ADVENTURES. FANTASTIC! EVEN THE MOST DEDICATED OF WALDO-WATCHERS AMONG YOU MAY HAVE TROUBLE RECOGNIZING ALL THE OLD FRIENDS HERE—IT'S QUITE A CHALLENGE. BUT HERE'S AN EASIER TEASER THAT ANYONE CAN DO: JUST LOOK AT THE CIRCLED FACES IN THE BORDER OF THIS FRAME, THEN SEE IF YOU CAN SPOT THEM IN THE SURROUNDING PICTURE.

EXHIBIT 7 — OLD FRIENDS AGAIN

IT'S ALWAYS NICE WHEN FRIENDS CAN STAY
A LITTLE LONGER. . . . HERE'S A COLLECTION OF
PORTRAITS OF SOME OF THE OLD FRIENDS FROM NEXT
DOOR — BUT IN SILHOUETTE FORM. CAN YOU MATCH UP
THE BLAST-FROM-THE-PAST CHARACTERS ON THE
PREVIOUS PAGE WITH THEIR SILHOUETTES HERE? JUST
TO MAKE IT INTERESTING, SOME OF THEM ARE UPSIDE
DOWN OR SIDEWAYS. SO, ONWARD AND UPWARD (AND
DOWNWARD AND SIDEWAYS!), PICTURE HUNTERS!

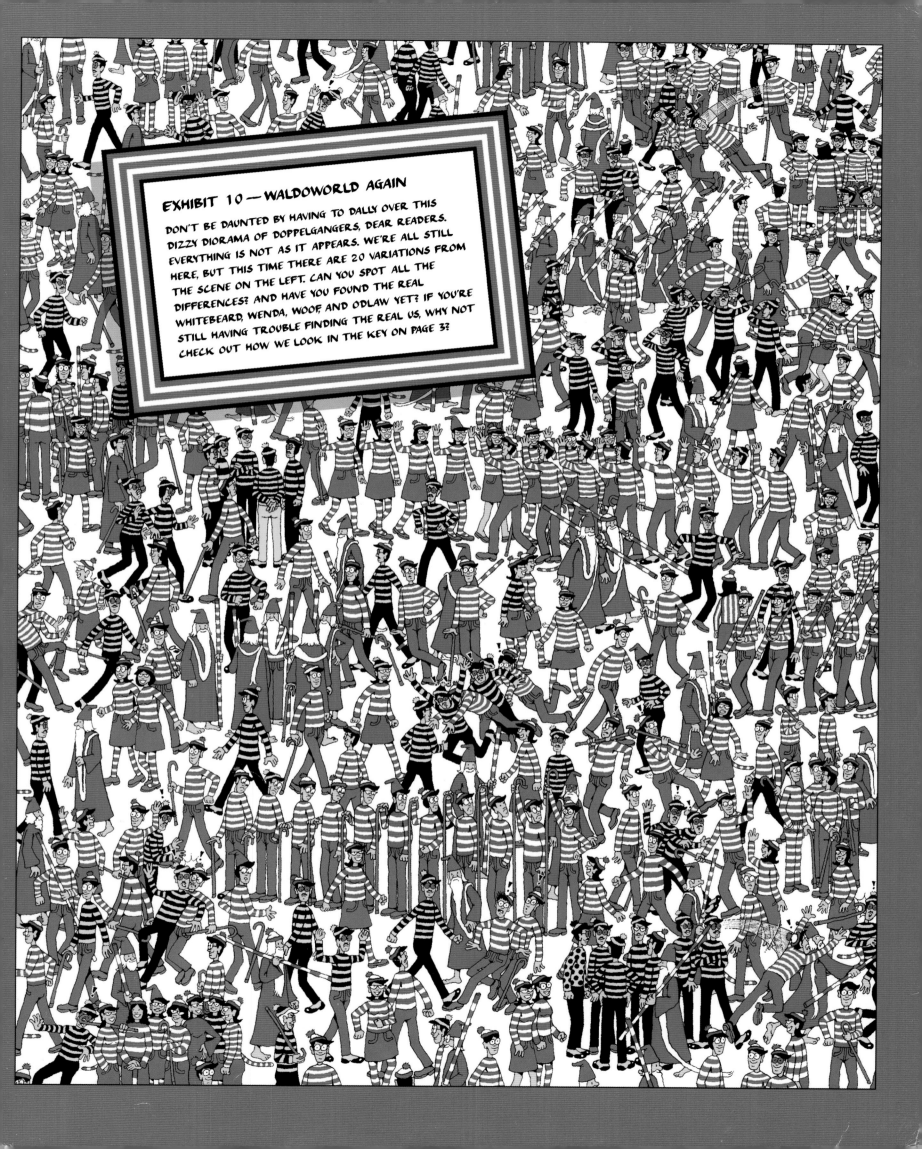

EXHIBIT 10 — WALDOWORLD AGAIN

DON'T BE DAUNTED BY HAVING TO DALLY OVER THIS DIZZY DIORAMA OF DOPPELGANGERS, DEAR READERS. EVERYTHING IS NOT AS IT APPEARS. WE'RE ALL STILL HERE, BUT THIS TIME THERE ARE 20 VARIATIONS FROM THE SCENE ON THE LEFT. CAN YOU SPOT ALL THE DIFFERENCES? AND HAVE YOU FOUND THE REAL WHITEBEARD, WENDA, WOOF AND ODLAW YET? IF YOU'RE STILL HAVING TROUBLE FINDING THE REAL US, WHY NOT CHECK OUT HOW WE LOOK IN THE KEY ON PAGE 3?

EXHIBIT 11 — PIRATE PANORAMA

SHIVER ME TIMBERS, SHIPMATES, WHAT PERFIDIOUS PIRATE PANORAMA IS THIS? WOW! AMAZING! WE'VE SAILED THE SEVEN SEAS SEARCHING FOR THOSE 30 PESKY PORTRAIT PEOPLE, AND NOW THAT OUR JOURNEY IS ALMOST OVER, I JUST HOPE THE PIRATES DON'T MAKE THEM WALK THE PLANK! I'M SURE THEY WOULD RATHER BE MAROONED ON A DESERT ISLAND THAN MEET THESE BARMY BUCCANEERS. ALL HANDS ON DECK!

EXHIBIT 12 — THE GREAT PORTRAIT EXHIBITION

OUR JOURNEY IS NOW OVER, WALDO FANS, BUT WHAT A FITTING
FINALE — A FANTASTIC EXHIBITION IN A PROPER ART GALLERY!
THE CROWD HERE SEEMS MORE WELCOMING THAN ODLAW'S ODD
ENSEMBLE FROM THE FIRST SCENE. I'M ALSO REALLY PLEASED
THAT ALL 30 OF THE CHARACTERS WE'VE BEEN SEARCHING
FOR IN THE EARLIER SCENES APPEAR AGAIN HERE AMONG THE
GALLERY GAZERS. SEE IF YOU CAN SPOT THEM AS THEY TRY TO
BLEND INTO THE CROWD AND ENJOY THE SHOW. I HOPE YOU
FOUND THEM IN THE PREVIOUS PAGES, TOO. IF NOT, THERE'S STILL
PLENTY OF TIME TO DO SO — THE EXHIBITION NEVER CLOSES!

WHERE'S WALDO?

THE GREAT PICTURE HUNT!

CHECKLISTS & ANSWERS

Lots more things for Waldo-watchers to look for!

EXHIBIT 1—ODLAW'S PICTURE PANDEMONI

- [ ] A green-skinned pirate
- [ ] Two ghost imposters
- [ ] Five mummies
- [ ] A bandaged finger
- [ ] Two spiders
- [ ] A head and crossbones
- [ ] A drooping flower
- [ ] Two teddy tattoos
- [ ] A black cat
- [ ] The sun
- [ ] Eight striped witches' hats
- [ ] Fourteen ladders
- [ ] Twelve vultures
- [ ] An upside-down skull and crossbones
- [ ] Four flying witches
- [ ] A pair of heart-shaped sunglas
- [ ] Three spike-topped helmets
- [ ] A puzzled, fangless vampire
- [ ] A drinking straw
- [ ] A squashed Viking

EXHIBIT 2—A SPORTING LIFE

- [ ] Hitting a hole in one
- [ ] A centaur circle
- [ ] A volleyball court
- [ ] Serving an ace
- [ ] A boxer saved by the belle
- [ ] Four under Pa
- [ ] The baseball batter's swing
- [ ] A pool table
- [ ] A Jim instructor
- [ ] Dancers at a soccer ball
- [ ] Team subs
- [ ] A marshal arts class
- [ ] Weight lifters pumping iron
- [ ] Shadowboxers
- [ ] A football quarterback
- [ ] Snow-peaked caps
- [ ] A pair of swimming trunks
- [ ] An archer with a long bow
- [ ] A steeplechase
- [ ] A pear skating

SPOT-THE-DIFFERENCES EXHIBIT 4— BROWN SAILORS AND GREEN SCALERS AGAIN ANSWERS

- [ ] A missing tail-end
- [ ] An absent cloud
- [ ] A brown balloon
- [ ] A balloon number missing
- [ ] A missing tooth
- [ ] A missing lasso
- [ ] Some smoke missing
- [ ] A missing flag
- [ ] A monster without spots
- [ ] A backward number
- [ ] A flag number missing
- [ ] A missing monster
- [ ] An absent sailor
- [ ] A missing telescope
- [ ] A man with a yellow beard
- [ ] Some missing green slime
- [ ] An extra sailor
- [ ] A slime gun without a nozzle
- [ ] A brown sea creature
- [ ] A sailor in a white top

EXHIBIT 5—THE PINK PARADISE PARTY

- [ ] Two skates on skates
- [ ] A broken heel
- [ ] A heavy-metal guitarist
- [ ] Two banana skins
- [ ] A pencil skirt
- [ ] Ball room dancers
- [ ] Two bugs jitterbugging
- [ ] A sole singer
- [ ] Dancers tripping on beads
- [ ] A Miniskirt
- [ ] A tea-shirt
- [ ] Two foxtrotters
- [ ] Platform shoes
- [ ] Some disc jockeys
- [ ] Oliver Twisting
- [ ] A Duke box and jukebox
- [ ] Dancing the knight away
- [ ] Beehive hairdos
- [ ] Squares square-dancing
- [ ] Two doormen

WELCOME, WALDO FANS, TO MY WONDERFUL WORLD OF STICKERS! HERE ARE FORTY FABULOUS FRAMES TO USE WHEN YOU PLAY THE GREAT PICTURE HUNT.

WHENEVER YOU FIND ONE OF THE THIRTY MISSING PORTRAIT SUBJECTS, YOU CAN PUT HIM OR HER BACK IN THE PICTURE BY FRAMING HIM OR HER WITH A STICKER.

DIDN'T FRAME IT JUST RIGHT? IF YOU'RE CAREFUL, YOU CAN PEEL UP THE STICKER AND REPOSITION IT, OR PLACE IT BACK HERE TO PLAY THE GAME AGAIN LATER.

I'VE ALSO INCLUDED A SELECTION OF STICKY PICS OF YOURS TRULY, MY FRIENDS, AND EVEN THAT SCOUNDREL ODLAW! BUT THESE STICKERS ARE FOR DECORATIVE PURPOSES ONLY — YOU CAN STICK THEM (ALMOST) ANYWHERE.

SO GET PEELING, STICKER PICKERS—THE FRAME GAME IS AFOOT!